I HATE
COMPANY

I HATE COMPANY

by P. J. Petersen
illustrated by Betsy James

DUTTON CHILDREN'S BOOKS
New York

Library of Congress Cataloging-in-Publication Data
Petersen, P. J.
I hate company / by P. J. Petersen; illustrated by Betsy James.
—1st ed.   p.   cm.
Summary: When his mother offers to share their apartment
temporarily with an old friend and her three-year-old son,
Dan finds himself resenting the loss of space, privacy, and
peace and quiet.
ISBN 0-525-45329-6
[1. Hospitality—Fiction.   2. Behavior—Fiction.
3. Apartment houses—Fiction.]   I. James, Betsy, ill.
II. Title.   PZ7.P44197Iac   1994
[Fic]—dc20   94-2801   CIP   AC

Published in the United States by Dutton Children's Books,
a division of Penguin Books USA Inc.
375 Hudson Street, New York, New York 10014
Designed by Carolyn Boschi
Printed in U.S.A.   First Edition
10 9 8 7 6 5 4 3 2 1

Reprinted by arrangement with Dutton Children's Books,
a division of Penguin Books USA Inc.

For Karen and Adam Harvey

P.J.P.

For the kids at
A:Shiwi and Dowa Yalanne elementary schools

B.J.

I HATE
COMPANY

Chapter 1

I hate company. I really do.

Mom doesn't like to have me use the word *hate*. She says it's an ugly word. But for some things, no other word will do. Like having an ant crawling on me. I hate that. The ant always gets under my shirt and goes scooting around on my bare skin. I yank off my shirt and try to grab it before it bites. And I'm always too late. I get shivers thinking about it.

And I hate to have guys sneak up behind me and grab me. They tiptoe up, then yell and dig their fingers into my ribs. I jump six feet in the air and scream. And they laugh like crazy and say, "Gotcha." Guys like that should have buckets of ants poured down their backs.

And I hate having my mother call me by all three of my names. When I hear her say "Daniel Edward Barton," I know that I'm in deep trouble. I hate it.

And I hate gum on my shoe. And bike tires that go flat. And dogs that jump all over me. And dog owners who let their dogs jump all over me and then say, "He likes you."

But, most of all, I hate company.

Not all company, of course. I love to have some guys sleep over at my place. We put our sleeping bags in front of the TV, and we eat popcorn and drink lemonade and watch movies.

And I don't really mind having relatives come over for dinner. Even ones like Aunt Doris and Uncle Ray, who pat me on the head and ask me dumb questions that don't have answers like, "When are you going to stop growing?" Or Great-aunt Martha, who takes out her false teeth and puts them on the table.

People like that are fine—just as long as they go home at night.

The company I hate are the ones who stay

overnight. Because they always take my bed and my room. Our apartment isn't very big—two bedrooms and a front room that's divided into a living room and a kitchen. But it's fine until we have company. Then it seems really little. Especially if the company stays in the bathroom for an hour.

. . .

So when Mom told me her friend Kay was coming—and bringing her three-year-old boy—my first question was: "How long are they going to stay?"

"I'm really excited," Mom said. "Kay and I have been friends since we were in Mrs. White's first grade class."

It was hard for me to think of Mom as a first grader. "How long is she staying?"

But Mom wasn't listening. "Kay and I used to eat paste. You know that white stuff that comes in big jars? We loved the taste of it."

"I don't think they have it anymore," I said.

Mom was smiling and looking up at the ceiling. "We only quit eating that stuff because a third grade boy told us it would make our insides stick together."

"Mom," I said, "how long is she staying?"

Mom took a long breath and let it out. "She's staying as long as she wants. She's getting a divorce, and she's coming here to look for a job. She won't get an apartment until she finds one."

"What if she doesn't find a job right away?" I asked.

"Listen, Dan," Mom said, "I know this isn't going to be easy for you. But Kay is my dear friend, and she needs our help right now. And I know you like to help other people."

What could I say to that? Sure, I like to help people. But I wished there was some way to help besides giving up my room.

Chapter 2

Kay was supposed to come on Saturday afternoon. So I spent the morning hiding my stuff in places a three-year-old wrecking machine couldn't find it.

I put my train and my helicopter behind the towels in the bathroom closet, and I put my Legos behind the pots in the kitchen cupboard.

I came out of my room with my arms full of books. "Mom," I said, "can I put these under your bed?"

Mom took a book off the pile. "*The Little Red Hen?* When's the last time you read this?"

"I don't want it wrecked," I said.

"Why not? You'll never read it again."

Mom was right. I hadn't opened that book since I was in the first grade. But I didn't want it messed up. I don't know why.

I ended up putting my books back in the bookcase. But my dump truck and my microscope went under Mom's bed. Also my baseball cards and two kites and the puppet I made in school.

"That's enough," Mom said. "You're turning my room into a landfill."

But later on I sneaked in some puzzles and my box of race cars.

While Mom and I waited for Kay, my friend Mark called and invited me to go to a movie. Mom said no. She wanted me home when Kay arrived. So I had to sit there and wait, knowing that I was missing a movie.

Then Amy, a girl who lives next door, came by. "Guess what!" she shouted. "Dad's taking us to a baseball game this afternoon, and he said you could come."

I looked at Mom, and she shook her head. "We're having company," I said.

"It's a doubleheader," Amy said. "Two games. And all kids get free baseball cards."

I wanted to scream and stamp my feet and yell, "I hate company!" I tried to say, "Have fun," but the words got stuck in my throat.

Mom and I waited and waited. Kay still hadn't come when Mark called to tell me about the movie. So I could have gone with him if we'd known. And the movie was great, of course. And I had to listen to Mark tell all the good parts.

When the doorbell finally rang, Mom ran out of our place and down the stairs. I came along behind her. She threw open the front door and shouted, "I'm so glad you're here."

Mom and Kay hugged each other and danced around. Both of them were talking at once. I didn't understand one word.

After a while, Mom stepped back and said, "You remember Aunt Kay, don't you?"

"Sure," I lied. I knew her voice from the phone, but that was all.

Kay stepped back and looked down at me. "This can't be Danny."

"Dan," I said.

Kay reached out her arms to me. "Come here and give me a hug."

She grabbed me and pulled me close. Her clothes had cigarette stink on them. Just what we needed—a smoker.

"Hi, Aunt Kay," I said.

She gave me another squeeze. "Oh, don't call me Aunt Kay. It makes me feel old. Just call me Kay, all right?"

"Where's Jimmy?" Mom asked her.

"In the car." Kay pointed to a white station wagon that was crammed full of cardboard boxes. "He stayed awake for four hundred miles, then went to sleep three blocks from here."

"Rough day?" Mom asked.

Kay laughed and put her arm around Mom. "It was awful. I thought I had a great idea. I had a box of stories on cassettes. But he only wanted *The Three Little Pigs*. Over and over. You can't believe it. Eight hours of 'Not by the hair on my chinny-chin-chin.' And he would *not* go to sleep." She looked down at me. "I'm sorry, Danny. Jimmy's going to be a holy terror tonight. He's awful when he's tired."

I tried to smile, but it was too much—a cigarette smoker and a holy terror.

We walked over to the car. There must have been twenty boxes inside. If we put all that stuff in my room, Kay and the kid would have to sleep on the couch with me.

Kay eased open the door and handed me a teddy bear. It was sopping wet. I almost dropped it. "It's not what you think," Kay said. "He's been chewing on it for four hundred miles."

I still held the bear with two fingers.

Kay slid Jimmy out of his car seat. Mom walked ahead of her and opened the doors. I came along behind with the soggy bear.

"You can put him on my bed for now," Mom whispered.

Kay laid Jimmy on Mom's bed and put pillows around him. She put the teddy bear next to his

head. Then we tiptoed out of the room. Kay closed the door softly. "He ought to sleep for hours," she said.

"You and Jimmy will be in here," Mom said, pointing at my room. "Just make yourself at home. This is your place now."

I looked at Kay. I hoped she didn't really believe that.

The door to Mom's room swung open just then. Jimmy stood there with his teddy bear in his arms. His black hair was sticking out in all directions. "I'm all done resting," he said.

"Don't you want to take a little nap?" Kay said.

Jimmy shook his head. "Nope."

"You've had a long day, honey."

"I'm all done resting," he said.

"All right, Jimmy," Kay said. "Say hi to Aunt Carol. And this is Danny."

"Dan," I said.

"Hi, Jimmy," Mom said.

Jimmy didn't even look at her. He walked over to me and said, "Hi, guy. You want a bear hug?" Before I could say anything, he grabbed me around the middle and went, "Gr-r-r-r-r-r."

"Do I get one?" Mom asked.

"Nope," Jimmy said. He grabbed me again and roared, "Gr-r-r-r-r-r."

For just a minute, I thought things might be okay. He was a cute little guy, and he liked me.

But the good times didn't last. In an hour my room was piled high with boxes, and we had *The Three Little Pigs* blasting from our tape player.

I was supposed to play with Jimmy, but the only game he liked was for me to pile up blocks for him to knock over. After the first thirty times, that game got a little old. But not as old as "Little pig, little pig, let me come in."

Mom and Kay were talking and giggling like little kids. Kay stood by the kitchen window with her cigarette and blew her smoke outside. But most of it blew back in.

"Jimmy," I whispered, "do you like TV?"

"I like the pigs," he said.

"Let's try the TV." I flipped off the tape player and turned on the TV. "There's a really good show on."

Jimmy stuck out his lip, and his big eyes filled with tears. "I like the pigs," he said. "Please. Please. Pleeeeease."

Mom looked my way. "Don't tease him, Dan."

I turned off the TV, flipped on the tape, stacked the blocks, and wondered how long they were going to stay.

Jimmy laughed out loud. "You want a bear hug?" He grabbed me and yelled, "Gr-r-r-r-r."

Chapter 3

The next morning Jimmy woke me up by sticking a crayon in my nose.

I would have been in a rotten mood anyway, but a nose full of crayon didn't help. The night before had been terrible.

Since I was sleeping on the couch, I figured I could watch the monster movies on late-night TV—which Mom never lets me do. If I kept the volume low, nobody would know. *Attack of the Tomato Worms* came on at eleven, and I was sure Mom would be in bed by then. I couldn't wait to tell the guys at school.

But Mom and Kay were still talking at eleven. And at twelve. So instead of watching a great movie, I had to listen to them laugh about people they went to school with. And I had to smell Kay's nasty cigarettes.

Usually I don't believe in hitting kids, especially little ones. But if a kid really asks for it, maybe it's not such a bad idea. And I figured that shoving crayons in noses was asking for it. I threw back my blankets and grabbed for Jimmy, but he dodged and ran to the kitchen, laughing the whole way.

Mom was sitting at the table, reading the newspaper. Jimmy got behind her chair and smiled at me. "Hi, guy," he said.

Mom looked my way. "Good morning."

"He shoved a crayon in my nose," I said.

Mom laughed. I could see how much help she was going to be.

"I want the pigs," Jimmy said. "Pleeeeease."

"Would you put on his tape?" Mom said. "He's been waiting a long time."

I looked at Mom. "You told him he couldn't

play his tape until I woke up, right? And he woke me up just so he could hear his stupid story."

Mom smiled. "He's three years old."

Jimmy held up three fingers. Then he reached over with his other hand and raised his little finger partway. "I'm three and a half."

"He's also a *b-r-a-t*," I said, starting for the bathroom.

"I want the pigs," Jimmy said.

"Play his tape for him, Dan," Mom said.

I put on the tape, and the little guy laughed. I could see who was going to be the boss around there.

On Sunday morning there are Roadrunner cartoons on Channel Eleven, but I had to listen to *The Three Little Pigs* instead. Jimmy lay on his stomach by the couch, scribbling in a coloring book. He had a big box of crayons, but he only used the green one. That was probably the one he shoved in my nose too.

He wasn't listening to the story at all, but

each time the tape finished, he'd yell, "I want the pigs." And Mom would smile at me, and I'd start the tape again.

After breakfast Mom sent me to the store for milk. I was glad to get out of there. Just as I started for the door, she said, "Maybe Jimmy wants to go."

Jimmy kept coloring. "Nope."

I didn't wait for him to change his mind.

On my way to the store, I saw Amy playing hopscotch by herself. "We saw two great games," she said. "Six home runs."

Why is it that the games you can't go to are always good ones? I hate that.

"Do you want to see my baseball cards?" she asked.

When I came back with the milk, Mom and Kay were sitting at the kitchen table. Kay smiled at me and said, "Good morning, Danny."

"Dan," I said. I caught a look from Mom and added, "Good morning."

I put the milk in the refrigerator. Suddenly I knew something was wrong. The apartment was too quiet. No "Little pig, little pig." No TV.

I looked toward the living room. No Jimmy.

"Is Jimmy asleep?" I asked.

Kay shook her head. "He doesn't take naps."

I ran for my bedroom. "What's the matter?" Mom asked.

Jimmy was sitting in front of my bookcase. He had his back to me, bent over a book. "What are you doing?" I asked.

Jimmy jumped up and dropped the book. "Mommy!" he yelled.

I reached down and grabbed the book. It was *The Little Red Hen*. Except now it might as well have been *The Big Green Blob*. He had scribbled all over the pages.

"You wrecked my book," I said, grabbing his arm.

"Mommeeeee," he screamed.

Kay and Mom were in the doorway before I could do anything. "Daniel," Mom said quietly.

I let go of Jimmy's arm. "The little brat wrecked my book," I said. Mom gave me one of her ice-cold looks.

Jimmy was rubbing his arm and saying, "Ouchie, ow. Ouchie, ow."

"I didn't hit him," I said.

Kay scooped up Jimmy and held him against her shoulder. "I'm sorry, Danny."

"It's nothing," Mom told her. "It's just an old book that Dan was ready to throw away."

"You know better than that," Kay told Jimmy. "You only color in coloring books and on special paper. Tell Danny you're sorry."

Jimmy pushed himself away from Kay's shoulder and looked at me. "You hurt my arm," he said, sticking out his lip and shaking a finger at me. "You're a bad boy."

Mom turned her back, but I knew she was laughing. She was a big help.

"Let's get your jacket on," Kay said. "I think you need a walk."

I went back to the living room and turned on the TV. I kept my eyes on the screen until Kay and Jimmy were gone.

As soon as the door closed, Mom walked over

and turned off the TV. "I think you can do better than that," she said.

"Come on, Mom, he's a brat."

Mom nodded. "He's acting that way right now. But that doesn't mean you have to do the same."

I didn't have anything to say to that.

"Jimmy's upset," Mom went on. "And Kay is having a hard time too. I want you to do everything you can to make things better for them."

"I can't stand that stupid *Three Little Pigs*," I said.

She nodded again. "It's not my favorite either, but we can put up with it. And I don't want you calling him names."

"I just said he was a brat. And he is."

"I'm serious," Mom said.

"I can't help what I think," I told her.

"No," she said. "But you can help what you say."

"I won't say anything," I said. "But I might think rotten stuff."

Mom smiled. "It'd be better if you didn't think those things, but nobody can read your mind."

So I put away my scribbled-on book, and I smiled.

"That's better," Mom said.

But she didn't know that I was thinking, *I hope they never come back.* In my mind I pictured a big bus picking up Kay and Jimmy and hauling them to the North Pole. And Jimmy colored the bus windows green.

A few minutes later Mom came over and gave me a hug. "You must be feeling better now."

"I am," I said. And that was true. I was picturing Jimmy sitting in an igloo. He was coloring the walls green.

NORTH POLE

WELCOME JIMMY!

Chapter 4

The next morning I didn't get a crayon up my nose. Jimmy took a flying leap and landed right on my stomach. I think I liked the crayon better.

Before I could do anything, he grabbed me around the neck and said, "You want a bear hug? Gr-r-r-r-r-r."

What could I do? It's hard to stay mad at somebody who's giggling and giving you a bear hug.

Besides, today was going to be a better day. I was going to school, so I wouldn't have to stack blocks. And I wouldn't have to listen to *The Three Little Pigs*.

Jimmy ate breakfast with me. I ate oatmeal, so he wanted oatmeal. Kay said he'd never liked it before. "He wants to be like you," she said. I had orange juice, so he wanted some. I had a banana, and he ate half of it. He brushed his teeth when I did, and he begged me to let him wear my baseball cap.

That gave me an idea. When we came out of the bathroom, I said, "I like to watch TV after breakfast. That's what big guys do."

Jimmy looked over at the TV. Then he looked back at me. "I like the pigs," he said. "Pleeeeease."

Usually when I come home from school, I stay with Mrs. Gray downstairs. But Mom said for me to come to the apartment. Kay was going to be there. "I'd rather stay with Mrs. Gray," I said.

Mom gave me that smile of hers.

"All right," I said. "I'll come home."

"I'll make you a deal," Mom said. "For the next few days you're going to be doing a lot of things you don't especially want to do. Be a good sport, and I'll do something I don't want to do—I'll take you to Star World."

Star World is this great amusement park north of the city. Mom hates the crowds, but I love the place. "It's a deal," I said. "I'll be the best sport you ever saw."

I came straight home after school. When I opened the door, the stink of cigarettes hit me in the face. But I didn't say a word. Kay was sitting at the kitchen table. She had a typewriter in front of her, with papers scattered all around.

"Hi, Danny," she said. "Jimmy's asleep."

"Hi," I whispered. The last thing I wanted to do was wake him up. I tiptoed over to the TV. I turned the sound all the way down before I hit the ON button.

A few minutes later Kay stood up. "Danny," she said, "I have to go down to the corner and make copies of these papers. Will you be all right?"

"No problem," I whispered.

"You're sure? I can wait until Jimmy wakes up."

"Listen," I said, "I'm not a little kid. I can handle things."

"All right." She gathered up her papers. "I don't think he'll wake up, but if he does, tell him I'll be right back."

"No problem," I said again.

Two minutes after she left, I heard a noise in my room. I hoped Jimmy was just turning over in bed.

Pretty soon my bedroom door opened. "Hi, guy!" Jimmy yelled. He came running over to me. "You want a bear hug?"

His lips were dark purple. "What happened to your mouth?" I asked.

Jimmy looked toward the kitchen, then said, "That juice is yucky."

"What juice?" I asked. Then I realized what he'd said. I jumped up from the couch. "Where'd you get it?"

Jimmy stepped back. "I'm a good boy."

I tried to keep my voice quiet. "Right. You're a good boy. You're my pal."

"You want a bear hug?" He reached out his arms for me.

"In a minute," I said. "First I want you to show

me where you got the juice." I took his hand. "Come on and show me, and I'll let you wear my cap."

He led me back into my room. "There." An old box of poster paints was open on the floor. "I don't want any more juice."

I grabbed the box and read the word on top. *Nontoxic*, it said. That sounded bad. I took Jimmy's hand and led him to the kitchen. "We need to make a phone call right now." I tried to keep my voice steady, but Jimmy looked scared.

Mom has a list of numbers right by the phone. I called Dr. Gordon's office. "Listen," I told the woman who answered, "a little boy has just drunk some paint."

"I'll get the nurse," the woman said.

Right away the nurse came on the line. "Did you say he drank paint?"

"Yes."

"Do you know what kind?"

"Poster paint," I said. "It has a word on the box that I can't read."

"Spell it for me."

31

"N-o-n-t-o-x-i-c."

"Nontoxic," the nurse said. "That's good."

"What do you mean?" I yelled.

"That means it's not poisonous. You see, *toxic* means poison. So *nontoxic* means not poison."

"You mean it won't hurt him?" I asked.

"That's right." She went on to tell me I'd done exactly the right thing, calling the doctor when I wasn't sure. But by then I was thinking about another problem.

"Excuse me," I said. "Do you know how to get purple paint off a kid's mouth?"

She laughed. "Not really. You might try brushing his teeth."

I hung up the phone and hauled Jimmy to the bathroom. I figured we only had a couple of minutes to get rid of the purple. He started to fuss about brushing his teeth, but I got out my toothbrush too. Then it was all right.

The brushing helped a little, but his lips were still purple. "Keep brushing," I told him. "I'll be right back." I ran to the kitchen and put some dish soap on a wet paper towel. When I came back, Jimmy was standing by the sink with his purple mouth wide open.

"Where's your toothbrush?" I asked.

"All gone," he said.

"Where?"

He shrugged his shoulders. "All gone."

"Look," I said, "it can't fly. Where'd it go?"

He looked toward the toilet. "All gone."

"Oh no," I said. "You didn't put the toothbrush in the toilet, did you?"

He let out a crazy laugh.

I handed him the soapy paper towel. "Here," I said. "Scrub your mouth with this." Then I got down on my knees and tried to look as far into the toilet as I could.

I looked up when I heard him giggle. He had rubbed the soap on his hair. Big bubbles were sliding down his forehead.

That's when Kay walked in. I was down on my knees with my head in the toilet. Jimmy was standing there with a purple mouth and a soapy head.

Kay stood in the doorway for a minute, shaking her head. Then she blurted out, "What are you doing?"

I couldn't think of an answer, but Jimmy did. "Playing," he said.

And then two good things happened: Kay laughed, and Jimmy's toothbrush fell out of his shirt.

"You want a bear hug?" Jimmy said.

Kay kept laughing. "Sure," she said. "Just don't kiss me right now."

Chapter 5

The next few days wore me out. I stacked the blocks about a thousand times, and I heard *The Three Little Pigs* until I knew every stupid word. I read Jimmy stories, but guess which story he wanted most often. "Why should I read *The Three Little Pigs?*" I asked him. "You can hear it on tape."

And you know what his answer was? "You want a bear hug?"

Jimmy and I raced cars and rolled the ball and played a hundred games of hide-and-seek, even though we only had about two places to hide. I'd finally get so tired that I'd flop down on the floor. And then he'd sneak up and jump on my stomach.

Mom took over sometimes. She read him

stories and played blocks. But Jimmy liked me better. "I want to play with Dan," he'd say. "Pleeeease."

Kay played with him too. And she tried to make him be good. She was always taking him into my room for a talk or for something she called "time-out." But he was just the same afterward.

I tried to be a good sport, just the way Mom wanted. I didn't hit Jimmy or call him a brat. And I even bought him a baseball cap like mine. The only time he took it off was in bed, and sometimes he wore it there.

I figured that Mom owed me at least two trips to Star World. Maybe three.

When things got tough, I played games in my mind. I pictured Jimmy in Australia. A kangaroo had him in her pouch and bounced him all around. And I pictured him in Africa, playing hide-and-seek with the monkeys. I didn't want anything bad to happen to him. I just wanted him away from our place. Far away.

. . .

After a while I didn't even care about Star World. I just wanted to be left alone. It was bad enough to have a little kid hanging on me all day, but things kept going wrong besides.

Like the hide-and-seek game. Jimmy would always run and hide under the table. Then I'd go in the kitchen and walk around for a while before I looked under there.

After he'd hidden in the same place about thirty times, I started adding a little fun to the game. I'd stomp into the kitchen and call out, "Where is he? Is he in the sink? Is he in the cupboard?" And I'd open the cupboard. "Is he in the refrigerator?" And I'd open the refrigerator. Jimmy would be under the table laughing and laughing.

It was just a funny little game. But then Mom found Jimmy crawling into the refrigerator. "Guess where he got that idea," Mom said.

And then there was my workbook. On Tuesday I brought my math workbook home so that I could finish some problems. I was sitting at the table doing the last ones when Jimmy came in. He shook his finger at me and said, "Bad boy."

I laughed. "What do you mean?"

But he wasn't laughing. He pointed at the workbook. "Writing in the book. Bad boy."

That was funny, but I tried not to laugh. I hate it when people laugh at me for saying something dumb. "This is a workbook, Jimmy. You're supposed to write in it." I showed him all the pages I'd done.

And, of course, I came back later and found that he'd attacked that workbook with his green crayon.

Everybody at school thought it was funny. Except my math teacher.

I should have known better with the pencil sharpener. Jimmy came by while I was sharpening my pencil, so I let him turn the handle. He liked doing it so much that I found two more pencils he could sharpen.

That was it, I thought. But Jimmy wasn't finished. Before anybody caught on, he had sharpened crayons, carrot sticks, a candle, even a toothbrush.

I didn't see anything wrong with having him help make our snack. I just let him spread peanut butter on crackers. It didn't seem like a big deal, and he loved helping.

But it turned out that he liked making snacks a lot better than he liked eating them. So when nobody was looking, he made cracker sandwiches and hid them. We found crackers under the couch pillows, in his bed, in the oven, in the refrigerator. You can't believe how many crackers there are in one dinky box.

And every time Mom came up with another sticky smashed cracker, she looked at me and shook her head.

One afternoon Kay took us to the playground. That should have been safe enough, but it was more of the same old thing.

On the way, Jimmy kept running ahead of us. "Don't get too far," Kay called. So, of course, he ran faster.

She didn't have to worry. Nobody would want him. I pictured him with a sign around his neck: KID FOR SALE. Then I thought of a better sign: WE'LL PAY YOU $100 TO TAKE HIM. But nobody would want him, not after they'd played hide-and-seek for five hours or sat on a peanut butter cracker.

When we got to the playground, Kay said, "I'll go over there in the shade and read. You boys have fun."

The only thing Jimmy wanted to do was go

down the little kids' slide, which was about as high as my head. "Watch me!" he yelled. "Watch me!"

So I watched, again and again.

He always held on to the sides so he wouldn't go too fast. "Don't be scared," I told him.

Pretty soon he was letting go and sliding faster. "Watch me!" he yelled every time.

Then he wanted me to go down the slide.

"I'm too big for the slide," I told him.

"Don't be scared," he said.

"I'm too big," I said.

"Don't be scared," he said. "Don't be scared."

So I had to go down once. I waited until nobody was around, then climbed the little ladder. But just as I got settled on the slide, two fifth graders showed up. "Hey, Barton," one of them yelled, "get off that baby slide."

That's the way things went when Jimmy was around.

A few minutes later a little kid came along and shoved Jimmy away from the ladder. "Get out of my way," the kid said. "Or I'll sock you."

Jimmy came running over to me with tears in his eyes. "He pushed me."

"Don't be scared," I said. "You tell him to watch out, or I'll sock *him*."

Jimmy went running back to the slide. "Watch out," he said. "Or he's gonna sock you." The kid took one look at me and ran off. Jimmy laughed and laughed.

In a few minutes we went over to the jungle gym. I was sitting on a bar, thinking about flying a helicopter, when I heard Jimmy say, "Watch out, or he's gonna sock you."

I laughed and turned that way. Jimmy was talking to Norman Sanders, the meanest guy in my school.

"Who's gonna sock me?" Norman asked, letting out a rotten laugh.

I ducked down, but I knew Jimmy was pointing right at me.

In no time at all Norman was twisting my arm and making me say that I loved to eat worms and banana slugs.

Jimmy tried to help me. He shook his finger in Norman's face and said, "You're a bad boy."

Actually that helped a little. Norman laughed so hard he forgot about twisting my arm for a minute. Then he went back to work. "Say you love Mary Jane Paulson."

Norman ran off when Kay came over. "Wait'll I tell everybody what you said," he yelled back.

And the next day he told the whole school, including Mary Jane Paulson.

Chapter 6

Somehow a whole week went by. Kay filled out papers and went for interviews, but she didn't find a job. A cloud of stinky smoke hung over our apartment. And Jimmy was still listening to *The Three Little Pigs*.

I got so sick of playing hide-and-seek that I started playing horsie. That was a dumb mistake. From then on, all Jimmy ever wanted to do was to hop on my back for a ride. Pretty soon I was begging him to play hide-and-seek, just to give my knees a rest.

Mom was looking tired too. She was used to walking into a room and plopping down in a chair. You don't do that with a little kid around.

Especially one like Jimmy. If you plopped down in a chair, you were likely to plop right on a peanut butter cracker or a half-chewed banana.

And Mom wasn't used to watching the floor. She was forever tripping over blocks or race cars. She always smiled afterward, but you could tell she had to work at it.

Once when Kay took Jimmy to my room for a time-out, I whispered to Mom, "He gets on your nerves, doesn't he?"

Mom smiled. "He's a good boy. He's just three and a half, that's all."

"But he gets on your nerves. I can tell."

"That's just the way things are," Mom said. "Anybody you're around all the time will get on your nerves."

I thought about that for a minute. "Does that include me?"

She laughed. "No way, Dan. It's different with your own family."

It made me wonder all the same. *She* got on *my* nerves sometimes. But I didn't tell her that.

· · ·

When I came home from school Monday afternoon, the smoke cloud was thicker than usual. Kay was walking around the kitchen with a pile of papers in her hand. "Danny," she said, "I hate to ask you, but Jimmy's asleep right now, and I have to get these things copied and mailed."

"Listen," I said, "don't worry. I know I messed up last week, but it won't happen again."

She waved me away. "You didn't mess up. It wasn't your fault Jimmy drank poster paint."

"Anyway, don't worry, I'll take care of everything."

"I'll only be gone about fifteen minutes. Twenty at the most. If you have any problems, Mrs. Gray is right downstairs."

"We'll be fine." I poured myself a glass of milk and turned on the TV, keeping the sound low.

The second that Kay closed the door, Jimmy came out of the bedroom. "Hi, guy," he said.

"Hi." I turned my back and finished my milk. I didn't want to give him any ideas about getting something to eat. I wanted to be sure nothing went wrong this time. I wasn't going to take chances with spilled juice or broken dishes.

"Let's play horsie," he said.

"Good idea." That was one way to keep him out of trouble. I got on my knees, and he climbed onto my back. I crawled into the living room, then back to the kitchen, then back to the living room.

"Go fast!" he yelled. "Go fast!"

When I couldn't go any farther, I stopped by

the kitchen table. "Horsie's tired," I said. "Let's play ball."

I got his little rubber ball, and we sat facing each other on the floor with our legs wide apart. I rolled the ball to him, and he grabbed it. "Good catch," I said.

I glanced at the clock. Kay had already been gone ten minutes. Five minutes of ball and another horsie ride, and she should be back.

We rolled the ball back and forth, a little faster each time. Then Jimmy picked up the ball and gave it a toss. It bounced over my leg and rolled under the refrigerator. "Just leave it," I said. "Let's play horsie again."

"I want my ball." Jimmy ran over and reached under the refrigerator. He came out with his ball, but he also came out with a big spot of black grease on his hand.

"Wait a second," I said, but he wiped his eye with the greasy hand. "Don't move. You've got grease on your hand."

Jimmy saw the grease and touched it with his

other hand. So both hands were black. I grabbed one of his hands, but he used the other to scratch his stomach.

I caught the other hand and lifted him off the ground. "All right," I said. "We're going to have a bath. We want to get this yucky stuff off you right now."

Jimmy liked baths, so he didn't argue. I put in some of his bubble bath and filled the tub. I managed to take off his clothes without spreading the grease much farther.

"I want my hat," he said.

So I let him keep his cap on.

The grease came off with a little scrubbing, and I was feeling a lot better. With any luck at all, I could have him out and dressed before Kay came back. "All right, out we come."

Jimmy stood up, then pulled away and sat on the back of the tub. "I do the slide."

"No!" I shouted. But it was too late. He zipped down and hit the water like a rock. Soapy water flew all over the bathroom.

I grabbed him and lifted him out of the tub, then wrapped him in a towel. "Just stand right there," I said. I got an old towel out of the cupboard and used it to mop the floor.

"Hide-and-seek!" Jimmy yelled. He ran out of the bathroom and slammed the door behind him. I went ahead and finished mopping.

Then I picked up his clothes and went after him. I didn't want Kay to come back and find him wearing a towel.

When I opened the bathroom door, I saw that Kay wouldn't find him in a towel. The towel was lying there on the floor.

"All right, Jimmy," I called, "let's get you dressed." I walked into the kitchen and looked under the table. He wasn't there. "All right, Jimmy. Time to get dressed."

I stopped and looked around. Everything was very quiet. Too quiet.

I ran to the living room and looked behind the chair. "Jimmy!" I dashed into Mom's room and looked in her closet and under her bed. Nothing there but my toys.

I threw open the door to my room. "Jimmy!" The room was empty.

I ran back to the kitchen and yanked open the door to the refrigerator.

Then the apartment door opened, and Kay walked in. "Look what I found on the front steps," she said.

There was Jimmy—wearing nothing but his baseball cap. "Hi, guy," he said.

Chapter 7

Things were worse the next few days. Along with the horsie rides and the hide-and-seek, I had to listen to Kay tell people about finding her naked kid on the street. It wasn't bad enough for her to tell Mom and Mrs. Gray and all the neighbors. She even called her mother in Los Angeles and told her.

So everybody got to laugh at me. The only good thing was that I didn't get left alone with Jimmy again. That made me happy in a way. But it made me mad too. I didn't like the idea that they thought I was too little and too dumb to take care of him.

Jimmy still woke up early every morning. Kay had tried to help by making him promise not to touch me. If he did, he couldn't wear his cap all day. So he didn't touch me. But he got his face about one inch from mine and kept it there. So the first thing I saw when I opened my eyes were two eyeballs staring back at me. That was as bad as a crayon in my nose.

Mom told me to teach Jimmy some new games. I showed him how to play fish, but the only card game he liked was fifty-two pickup. (You know that game? You throw the fifty-two cards, then pick them up. But the way Jimmy liked to play was for him to throw and me to pick up.)

I got a blanket and made a tent for him. He liked that—for about ten minutes. Then he wanted to play horsie again.

Sometimes when Kay was there in the afternoon, I'd go into Mom's bedroom and lock the door, just to be by myself for a while. But Jimmy would stand outside and knock and beg me to come out and play with him. "Please," he'd call. "Pleeeeeeeease."

Kay would take him away and try to get him

to color or something, but in two minutes he'd be back banging on the door. So I couldn't enjoy it.

By Sunday I couldn't stand any more. And Mom knew it. "You get a special treat," she told me. "There's a space movie called 2001 on Channel Eleven tonight. If you take a nap this afternoon, you can stay up and watch it."

She took Jimmy to the park so that I could sleep. I couldn't fall asleep anyway, but I didn't tell Mom that.

Kay put Jimmy to bed early, and I settled in to watch my movie.

Five minutes after the movie started, Jimmy poked his head out of the bedroom. "I want a drink of water," he said.

"Go get one and hurry back to bed," Kay told him.

He got his drink of water, then sneaked in by me. "Hi, guy."

"Be quiet," I said. "This is a good movie."

He sat for about thirty seconds, then said, "You want to play horsie?"

"Quiet."

"You want a bear hug?" He grabbed me around the neck. "Gr-r-r-r-r."

"Jimmy, go back to bed," Kay called out.

And of course he didn't go. So she got up and took him, and he cried and fussed.

Ten minutes later he was back. "Bug in my bed," he yelled. "Bug in my bed."

Kay checked his bed and didn't find anything, of course. But by then he was on the couch with me. "I want to see the show," he whined. "Please."

Then his tummy hurt. And he had to go potty. And he was thirsty. And he was hot.

It was my special movie—and I got to stay up until eleven to see it—but with Jimmy in and out, I couldn't figure out what was happening. I wouldn't have known the movie was over if THE END hadn't flashed on the screen.

I wanted to kick something. Or, better yet, somebody.

I was so mad I couldn't sleep for a long time.

Then I must have drifted off, because I woke up in the dark.

I smelled smoke. I jumped up, thinking the apartment was on fire. Then I saw the red glow of Kay's cigarette. She was sitting at the kitchen table.

That was too much. I'd been a good sport long enough.

I threw back my blankets and stomped into the kitchen. "I've had it!" I shouted.

I hit the light switch. "I can't stand—" I stopped when I saw Kay. She was sitting by the open window with tears running down her face.

"I'm sorry if I woke you, Danny."

I stood and stared at her. Finally I asked, "Are you all right?"

"I'm just having a cry," she said. "I'll be okay."

"Oh." I didn't know what else to say.

"Would you mind turning off the light?" she said. "It hurts my eyes."

I flipped the switch and started back for the couch.

"Don't go," she said. "We need to talk."

"We can wait till later."

"No, Danny. Come on over."

I went and sat in one of the kitchen chairs.

"I know it's hard on you. Sleeping on the couch. Having Jimmy in the way all the time. Having no time with your mom. I know it's hard."

She was exactly right, but I couldn't really say that. "It's okay."

"It's not okay," she said. "But you've been great, Danny. I want to thank you for being such a good friend. And right now Jimmy and I need all the friends we can get."

"Mmm," I mumbled. I felt bad about yelling at her, but I didn't know how to tell her that.

"And Danny," she went on, "if there's anything I can do to make things better for you, please tell me. I mean it."

Well, she had asked me. "One thing," I said. "Could you call me Dan?"

Kay laughed. "Sure. I keep trying to remember. You're too old to be called Danny, right?"

"Right." I stopped for a second, trying to think of the right words. I couldn't think of them, but I went ahead anyway. "And one other thing. I mean, I don't want you to get mad or anything."

"Go ahead and say it, Dan."

"I can't stand your cigarettes. They stink up the whole place so that I can hardly breathe."

I could tell that surprised her. "Really? I

thought with the window open—" She reached for an ashtray and ground out her cigarette.

We sat there for a long time. Then I said, "I guess I'll go back to bed." I got up from my chair.

"Dan," she said, "before you go, maybe you can do one thing for me."

"Sure."

She reached out her arms. "Come here and give me a bear hug."

Her clothes were full of smoke, but that time I didn't mind.

"Now go to bed. I'm all through crying. I have plenty to be thankful for—a place to stay and good friends. If I can just find a job, everything's going to be okay."

That gave me a great idea. I don't know why I hadn't thought of it sooner.

I went back to the couch feeling a lot better. I knew how to solve everybody's problems now. All I had to do was find a job for Kay.

Chapter 8

At breakfast, I asked Mom what kind of job Kay was looking for. "In Los Angeles, she worked for a department store," Mom said.

That seemed easy enough. I had seen two or three stores right in our neighborhood that had HELP WANTED signs in their windows.

It seemed to me that Kay didn't know much about looking for a job. Most of the time she was typing letters and making phone calls. She should have gone right out and asked for jobs. Maybe she was bashful.

Well, I wasn't bashful. This afternoon I'd go see what I could do. And if things worked out,

I'd soon be back in my own room, and Jimmy would be sticking things in somebody else's nose.

When I came home from school, Jimmy was playing drums with a big pot. "Boom, boom," he yelled while he smacked the pot with a spoon.

I set my backpack by the door and realized that something was different—the air was clear. "It smells good in here," I said.

Kay looked up from her typewriter. "Hi, Dan."

Jimmy came running over and gave me a bear hug. "Gr-r-r-r-r," he growled.

"I have to go out for a while," I told Kay.

Kay pushed herself away from the table. "Dan," she said, "I need a big favor." Then she smiled. "Another big favor."

"Sure," I said.

"Could you take Jimmy with you? He needs to get outside, but I've been waiting for a phone call. The man from Big T Stores said he'd call today."

"Does he have a job for you?"

"I was hoping so." She looked at her watch. "Now I'm afraid he's going to say no."

"Don't worry," I told her. "I think things will be okay." I took two bananas from the fruit bowl and peeled one for Jimmy. "Let's go, buddy."

Jimmy and I stopped first at the grocery store. I pushed open the door and asked Mr. Chung, "Do you have a job for somebody?"

Mr. Chung smiled and shook his head. "You come back when you're a little older."

"It's not for me," I said. But he had turned away and was ringing up groceries.

When we went into the bakery next door, Jimmy let out a squeal. "Donuts!" he yelled.

"You haven't finished your banana," I said.

He shoved the rest of his banana into his mouth. Then he ran to the glass cases. "I like this kind." He put his hand on the case, making a big banana smear of a handprint. "And this kind. And this kind."

The baker came out and looked down at the

banana smears on his case. "Can I help you?" he asked me.

"I like this kind!" Jimmy yelled, leaving another smear on the glass.

I grabbed his hand and pulled him back. "Do you have any jobs?" I asked.

Jimmy twisted away from me and ran to another case. "Cupcakes!" He put both hands on the case and pressed his nose into the glass.

The baker punched the cash register and took out a quarter. "Here you go, kid. Your job is to take your little brother somewhere else."

I hauled Jimmy outside. "But I want a donut," he said. "Please. Pleeeease."

"Let's play horsie," I said. I carried him piggyback down the block, looking for HELP WANTED signs in the windows.

"Faster," he said. "Go faster."

Around the corner we saw Amy. "Amy," I called, "will you do me a favor?"

"Maybe."

"This is Jimmy." I set Jimmy down. "I'm trying

to find a job for his mom, but he's slowing me down. I'll give you a quarter if you'll take care of him."

"But I want to go with you," Jimmy said. "Please. Pleeeeease."

I handed Amy the quarter. "You'd better come back soon," she said. I took off running and didn't look back.

I tried the hardware store and the music store and the frame shop. I was careful how I asked: "I know a woman who needs a job. Do you have one?"

They all said no, but the woman in the frame shop said the ice cream store needed help. So I ran straight to the ice cream store. What a great place that would be to work! Maybe Jimmy and I could visit her once in a while.

A woman in a striped apron smiled at me when I came inside. "Hello," I said. "I know a woman who needs a job. The woman at the frame store said you might need somebody."

"I sure do," the woman said. "Two of my girls quit."

"My mom's friend Kay really needs a job."

"What's she like?" the woman asked.

I thought for a second, wanting to say exactly the right thing. "She's a hard worker, and she's smart and nice."

I knew I'd done it right when the woman smiled. "She sounds perfect," she said. "You tell her to come see me."

"She can come right now," I said.

"That's just fine."

I went racing out of the store. I felt great. Kay would be so happy. And I'd get my room back. And maybe once in a while Kay would give me an ice-cream cone.

When I got back to the corner, Amy and Jimmy were playing hopscotch. "Hi, guy," Jimmy yelled.

"I found his mom a great job," I told Amy.

"That didn't take long," Amy said. "Jimmy was a good boy. I used the quarter to buy him a day-old donut, and he was fine."

I knelt down, and Jimmy climbed on my back. "You bought him a donut?"

70

She nodded. "But the baker was really a grouch. He must be having a bad day."

I ran all the way back to the apartment. I threw open the door and yelled, "Kay, I have a surprise for you!"

"Surprise!" Jimmy yelled, sliding down my back.

"Good," Kay said. "I love surprises."

"We found you a job," I said.

Kay gave me a funny look. "Isn't that nice. What kind of job?"

"It's great," I told her. "It's at the ice cream store."

Kay came over and wrapped an arm around each of us and said, "You're the sweetest boys in the world."

"You'd better get over there," I said.

Kay looked at the phone. "I'm still waiting for that call."

"I told the woman you'd come right away. She's expecting you."

Kay started to say something, then stopped. "All right," she said quietly. "Will you stay here and answer the phone? If somebody calls, be sure to ask if there's a message."

She and Jimmy left right away. She wasn't as excited as I thought she'd be, but I figured things would be different once she actually had the job.

A minute later the phone rang. A man asked for Kay, and I said she wasn't there. "Can I take a message?"

"This is Mr. Johnson at Big T Stores," he said. "We'd like her to come for another interview."

"I'll tell her," I said. "But I don't think she's interested anymore. She's just about to get a great job."

"Is that right?"

"Yes," I said. "They say she's perfect for the job."

"I see," Mr. Johnson said quietly. "Would you ask her to call me the minute she comes in? Tell her it's very important." He gave me a phone number, and I wrote it down.

· · ·

When Mom came in, I jumped up and ran to her. "Guess what? I found Kay a job. It's at the ice cream store. She's over there talking to the woman right now."

Mom gave me a hug, but I could tell something was wrong. I went ahead and told her the whole thing.

"Dan," she said, "that's really nice of you. But it's not the kind of job Kay's looking for."

That made me mad. "What? What's wrong with the ice cream store?"

"Kay works with computers," Mom said. "She handles all the bills for big stores."

"She could do ice cream, couldn't she?"

"Sure. But she'll make lots more money working with computers." Mom grabbed me and gave me another hug. "But you're so nice to try to help."

So that was it. I'd set out to do something good, and I'd ended up doing something stupid. And, worse than that, I'd probably messed up Kay's chances for the other job.

Chapter 9

When Kay came back, she said, "Thanks, Dan. We had a nice talk and a great ice-cream cone."

I told her the man from Big T Stores had called and wanted her to call him. I didn't tell her what I'd said to him. "I'll take Jimmy outside to play," I said. I didn't want to be there when she got the bad news.

"I want a donut," Jimmy said while he ran down the stairs. "Please." I pictured him in Antarctica. He and the penguins were eating donuts and playing horsie on the ice.

Amy was out in front of her building. Jimmy ran to her. "Hi, guy."

"I'm not a guy," Amy said. "I'm a girl."

"I want some more donuts," Jimmy said.

"How about some gum?" Amy held out a pack.

"Does your mom let you have gum?" I asked him.

He didn't answer me. He grabbed the gum and stuck it in his mouth.

"Just don't swallow it," I told him. I remembered Mom's story about the paste. "If you swallow gum, it makes your insides stick together."

We played hopscotch for a while, and Amy won. She always won at hopscotch.

When it was Jimmy's turn, he opened his mouth wide before he jumped. I realized that he didn't have his gum.

"Jimmy," I said, "where's your gum?"

"All gone."

"Did you eat it?"

He laughed. "I didn't eat it."

I looked around. "Did you throw it on the ground?"

He laughed again. "No."

"Then where is it?"

"I'll chew it some more after while," he said.

"But where is it now?" Amy asked him.

He smiled. "All gone."

I tried another way. "He doesn't know where it is," I told Amy.

"Do too."

"No, you don't."

"It's in my hat!" he yelled.

"Oh no," Amy moaned.

Some of the gum was in Jimmy's cap. But most of it was in his hair. Amy and I tried to pull it out, but Jimmy started to howl, "Ouchie ow, ouchie ow!"

I didn't know what to do. I hated to take him home that way. Things were bad enough already.

"We'll have to cut it out," Amy said. "That's what my mom did with me. I had eight pieces of gum, and I blew this big bubble. It popped and got all over my hair, and Mom had to cut it out."

"I wish we had some scissors," I said.

Amy went to her place and got scissors. "I didn't tell Mom," she said. "She might not want me to take her good scissors outside."

"Let me do it," I said.

Amy shook her head. "They're my scissors." She sat Jimmy on a step. Then she lifted up some of his hair and cut it off.

"Don't cut too much," I told her.

"I don't want a haircut," Jimmy said. "I want to go home."

"This will be fun," Amy told him. She snipped off some hair. Then some more. And some more. "That's it," she said. "I got out every bit of gum."

But Jimmy looked funny. He had white patches where she'd cut. "You cut too much in those places," I said.

"I had to get out the gum," she said.

"Let me have the scissors," I said. "I'll just even it out a little."

Amy handed me the scissors. "If you mess it up, it's not my fault."

I tried to cut just a little at a time, but I made some more white places.

Amy grabbed the scissors out of my hand. "You're making a mess." She made some more cuts, and Jimmy had even more white places.

"I want to go home," he said.

I wanted to go home too, but Jimmy's hair still didn't look right. "Maybe we could shorten it all over." I took the scissors and made some little cuts.

"You're making it worse," Amy said.

I handed her the scissors. "Then you do it."

Amy snipped a little hair here and a little there. Pretty soon Jimmy's head was full of white patches. Amy stepped back and looked at him. Then she said, "I have to go home now. It's dinnertime."

"Wait a minute," I said. "We're not done."

Amy started up the steps. "This was your idea. If you get in trouble, it's not my fault."

"Come back here with those scissors," I said.

Amy pulled open the door. "I have to eat dinner."

"But we're not done."

She looked down at us. "Yes, we are. He doesn't have any hair left." She went through the door. "And it was your idea."

I looked at Jimmy's fuzzy head. Amy was right. There wasn't much left to cut.

Jimmy started to sniffle. "I want to go home."

I looked at him, and I felt like crying too. "Put on your cap," I said.

I was really scared going home. Mom was going to take one look at Jimmy and yell "Daniel Edward Barton!" And I wouldn't have any excuse at all.

"I want a horsie," Jimmy said.

I didn't mind carrying him. At least that way I didn't have to look at his hair.

I carried him up the stairs and set him down in front of our door. I could hear Kay screaming inside.

For a second I thought about taking Jimmy away again. But I decided Kay might as well get all the bad things over with at one time.

I'm kind of ashamed to tell you, but I did a really chicken thing: I took off Jimmy's cap, shoved him inside, and shut the door again.

Then Kay really screamed. "Jimmy!" she shouted. "Come here to Mommy!"

The door flew open. Before I could move, Mom grabbed my arm and pulled me inside.

I had my eyes on the floor and didn't look at Mom. So the first thing I saw was Kay dancing around the kitchen, holding Jimmy in a big bear hug. "Dan, you're the greatest!" she shouted.

I stood there with my mouth open.

"You made him think I had another job," she said. "So he offered me the job right then. No more interviews. And a hundred dollars more a month than he said before." Still holding Jimmy, she came over and hugged me. "And all because of you."

"Making a sandwich," Jimmy said.

"That's right," Kay said. "A Jimmy sandwich." She kissed him on the top of his head. Then she leaned her head back and looked down at him.

"I'm sorry about his hair," I said.

"It's okay, Dan." She laughed and squeezed my shoulder. Then she stepped back and held Jimmy out in front of her. "Makes you look like a tough guy," she said to him.

"I didn't mean to—" I started.

Kay grabbed me and pulled me close again. "I know exactly what happened. He got gum in

his hair, and you cut it out. And then you tried to even things out." She shook her head and laughed. Jimmy laughed too.

"How did you know?" I asked.

"I did the same thing to my little brother," she said.

"I'm sorry," I said.

"Don't be," Kay said. "It's kind of cute, and it'll grow out. And I have a great job." She moved us over and hugged Mom too. "And I love all of you."

We stood there laughing and hugging—one big sandwich.

Chapter 10

Kay found an apartment the next day, and right away she started moving boxes and buying furniture. She seemed to be in a real hurry. She said she was excited about getting set up in her own place, but I figured she was tired of being company.

By Saturday she and Jimmy and all the boxes were gone. I had my dump truck and my microscope back on my shelf and my baseball cards back on my dresser. I still couldn't remember where I'd hidden my helicopter, but I figured I'd find it pretty soon.

I woke up by myself that morning. In my own bed. No crayons up my nose, no flying leaps onto my stomach. Then I spent the whole morning lying around watching cartoons.

I loved watching what I wanted. And lying wherever I wanted, with nobody climbing on me. And I loved the quiet.

But along about three in the afternoon, I started wondering what Jimmy was doing. His new place was on the other side of the city. I wondered if he'd found somebody to play with over there.

And just for a minute, the apartment seemed too quiet.

Don't get me wrong. I didn't want them to move back in. I was glad they were gone. But I guess I was kind of used to having them around.

I hate that. I wish things could be either one way or the other—all good or all bad. I hate that in-between stuff.

I was glad to have my old room back. And I was glad to have the bathroom free. And I was glad to stretch out and watch a whole TV show. But once in a while I wished Jimmy could come in—just for a minute—and say, "Hi, guy."

I walked to the kitchen. Mom was sitting at

the table, writing checks. "Well," she said, "are you enjoying the peace and quiet?"

"Yeah," I said. "But it's almost too quiet. You know what I mean?"

"Sure," she said. "You're glad they're gone, but you miss them."

"Does that sound dumb?"

Mom laughed. "Maybe. But that's the way things are sometimes."

"Hey, Mom," I said, "you want a bear hug?" I grabbed her around the neck and gave her a squeeze. "Gr-r-r-r-r."